# The Market Bowl

## Jim Averbeck

Charlesbridge

For the *Stage de Fête* and all our Cameroonian friends and colleagues.
With special thanks to Ed for putting up with me, and Helen and Gene
for putting me up. And thanks to Nathalie Mvondo and Luc Nya.

Published by Charlesbridge, 85 Main Street, Watertown, MA 02472, (617) 926-0329
www.charlesbridge.com

Library of Congress Cataloging-in-Publication Data
Averbeck, Jim.
   The market bowl / Jim Averbeck.
      p. cm.
   Summary: In this tale from Cameroon, Yoyo has to make amends when she offends
Brother Coin, the Great Spirit of the Market, by asking too high a price for her bitterleaf
stew. Includes a recipe for a version of bitterleaf stew.
   ISBN 978-1-58089-368-8 (reinforced for library use)
1. Fairness—Juvenile fiction. 2. Markets—Cameroon—Juvenile fiction. 3. Stews—
Juvenile fiction. 4. Cameroon-Juvenile fiction. [1. Fairness—Fiction. 2. Markets—Fiction.
3. Stews—Fiction. 4. Cameroon—Fiction.] I. Title.
PZ7.A933816 Mar 2013
813.6—dc23            2012007491

Printed in Singapore
(hc)  10 9 8 7 6 5 4 3 2 1

Illustrations done in acrylic paint and printed papers, scanned
   and assembled in Photoshop
Display type set in P22 Mayflower and text type set
   in Adobe Caslon
Color separations by KHL Chroma Graphics, Singapore
Printed and bound September 2012 by Inago in Singapore
Production supervision by Brian G. Walker
Designed by Susan Mallory Sherman

# PRONUNCIATION GUIDE

**Doula** (doo-AH-lah) The largest city in Cameroon; the name given to the ethnic group
of people who reside on the Atlantic coast of Cameroon; also *Duala*

*egusi* (eh-GOO-see) pumpkin seeds

*ndolé* (n-DOH-lay) bitterleaf stew

*njanga* (n-JAHN-gah) shrimp

*say-fah* phonetic spelling for French pronunciation of CFA,
or African franc

**Mama Cécile** sang to Yoyo, teaching her to make bitterleaf stew.

*"Slice the bitterleaf thin as a whisper.*
*Wash it in water, cleaning it well.*
*Grind the* egusi. *Add a knuckle of* njanga.
*Simmer some time for a fine stew to sell."*

"Mama, please," Yoyo said. "I can make my own stew. I am not a baby."

After all, she was finally old enough to sit on the seller's stool at market—if they ever got there. Slicing and grinding and measuring took too long!

So Yoyo didn't slice the bitterleaf nor grind the pumpkin seeds. *People just chew everything up anyway,* she thought. As for the *njanga,* she tossed in a whole bag of the salty dried shrimp.

After her pot cooled, Yoyo showed off her creation.

"Oh, child!" Mama Cécile gasped. "First tries are hard. You'll do better tomorrow. Best leave that for the goats."

The goats! Yoyo stuck out her proud chin. She was quite pleased with her stew, so she hid it deep in the market basket.

"Can we go now?" Yoyo asked.

"Breakfast first," Mama Cécile said.

Mama Cécile scooped out two helpings of her bitterleaf stew and, as always, asked the ancestors for a blessing on the food.

After breakfast she pulled out an enameled tin bowl.

"Yoyo, this is our market bowl, where we collect the money people pay for our stew. You must never, ever, refuse a fair price. If you do—"

"I know, Mama," Yoyo interrupted. "Brother Coin, Great Spirit of the Market, will be so angry he'll remove his blessing from our bowl. Let's go!"

At market Mama Cécile called out, "Bitterleaf stew! Fifty-fifty *say-fah* a bowl!"

Familiar faces lined up for a friendly chat and a scoop of Mama Cécile's stew. Coin after coin rang into the market bowl, until her stew pot was empty. She slipped behind the market stall to wash the dishes.

But one more buyer arrived.

Yoyo saw her chance. She leaped onto the seller's stool and scooped some of *her* stew for the stranger.

He scratched his head.

"Bitterleaf?" he asked, sniffing the stew. "Now, dis one—how much?"

"Fifty-fifty," answered Yoyo.

"Hmph. I give ten-ten." He held out two small coins.

"Ten-ten!" huffed Yoyo. "An insult!"

She snatched back the market bowl, just as his money dropped. The coins landed with a thud. A rumble of thunder rolled across the clear sky.

"Oh, Yoyo!" Mama Cécile cried. "What have you done?"

Weeks went by, but they sold not one spoonful more of bitterleaf stew. Each day their market bowl was empty.

Mama Cécile never sang anymore. She just wrung her hands and said, "How will we make a living?"

Each evening Yoyo dumped the spoiled stew.

Only the goats were happy.

As she watched them eat, Yoyo thought, *Why was the stranger so cheap?*

But then she thought some more. *My bitterleaf stew was awfully clumpy. And salty. And burnt. Maybe ten* say-fah *was a fair price.*

Yoyo squared her shoulders. "I'll make Brother Coin restore his blessing on our bowl."

Early the next day she took the market bowl, the ten *say-fah*,
and a paper twist of dried shrimp to munch on the way and set out
to find Brother Coin.

At the bush-taxi stand, the drivers called out their destinations:

"Douala!"

"Kribi!"

"Limbé!"

Yoyo approached a lone taximan. "I want to go to Brother Coin,"
she said. "I have ten *say-fah*."

"Tssst." The taximan sucked air through his teeth in disapproval
but added, "For ten *say-fah*, you ride with the luggage."

*It's a fair price,* thought Yoyo.

The taxi dropped Yoyo at an abandoned village near a shadowy cave.

"Good luck," the taximan said. "You'll need it."

Yoyo stole to the cave and peeked inside. Seated on an enormous throne was the equally enormous Brother Coin. At his feet an old man knelt with his market bowl.

"WHAT?" boomed Brother Coin.

"P-p-p-lease, sir," the old man stammered. "Restore your blessing on my bowl. . . ."

"After you broke my rules?" Brother Coin roared. "Begone!"

He snapped his fingers, and the man disappeared in a puff of smoke. The man's bowl flew through the air and landed on a pile of others with a clang.

Yoyo trembled. *How will I ever recover the blessing for Mama's bowl?* she thought.

Then she had an idea. She crept toward the village and scoured the area for what she needed.

Once she had found everything, Yoyo built a three-stone fire and placed her market bowl on top. This meal had to be fit for a god. Remembering Mama's song, she sliced the bitterleaf whisper-thin, then added *egusi* ground fine with a stone. But she added *two* knuckles of *njanga* because she liked things a little salty.

Soon the scent of simmering stew drifted toward the cave.

A divine belly rumbled within.

When the bitterleaf was ready, Yoyo tensed her knees to stop them from knocking, then strode into the cave.

"What do you want?" Brother Coin thundered. "I am granting no wishes today."

"Great Brother Coin," Yoyo called, "I came to offer this humble dish to your magnificent spirit."

"Bitterleaf?" Brother Coin drooled, smacking his lips.

"Yes," replied Yoyo, "the finest in all the province."

Brother Coin snapped his fingers. A silver spoon appeared in his hand. He grabbed for the bowl.

"Wait!" cried Yoyo.

Brother Coin's eyes narrowed.

"Mama Cécile says we must never eat without first asking for a blessing on our food," Yoyo scolded.

"Ha! She is right, little one," Brother Coin boomed. "But Brother Coin doesn't ask for a blessing; he gives it." With a wave of his spoon, he quickly intoned, "Bless this dish," then gobbled up the stew.

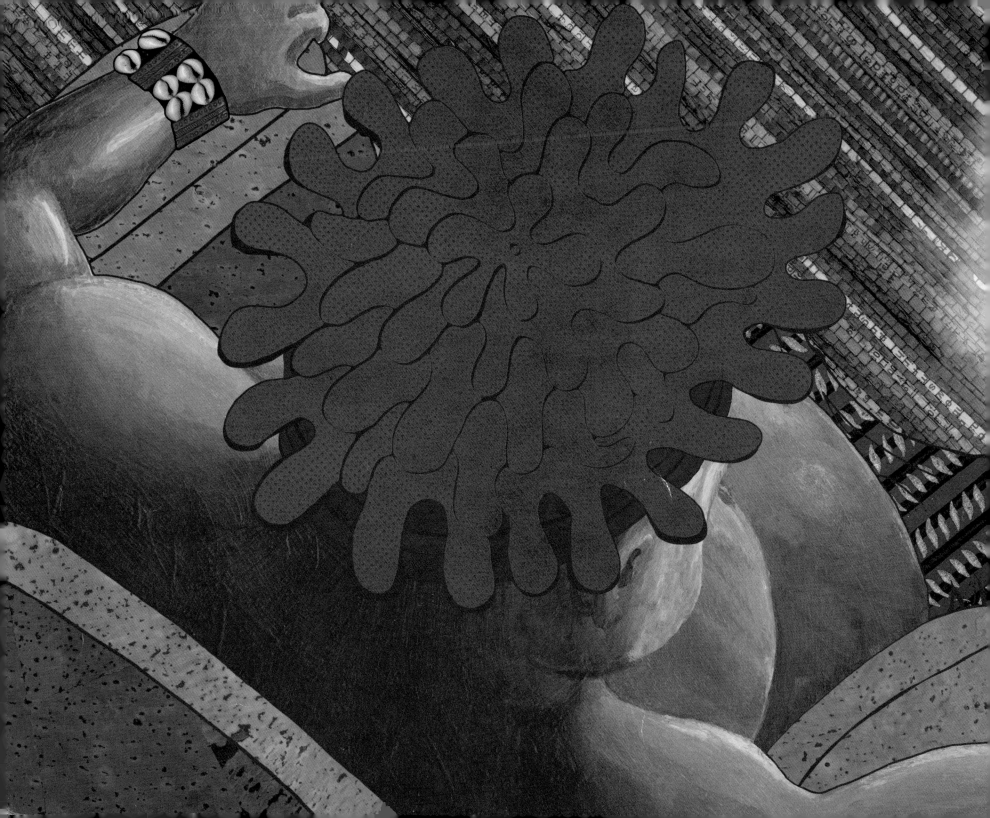

When he was finished, Brother Coin burped contentedly.

"Still here, little one?" He scowled at Yoyo. "I told you—no wishes today. Begone!"

He shoved the empty bowl into her hands. Yoyo hugged it to her heart.

*Snap!*

Yoyo found herself back in Mama Cécile's kitchen.

"There you are, child," Mama Cécile said. "Come prepare for market. Let's hope our stew sells today."

Indeed it did sell. And even though creating the finest bitterleaf stew meant spending all morning slicing and grinding and measuring . . .

Yoyo thought, *It's a fair price.*

## AUTHOR'S NOTE

Located in west-central Africa, Cameroon is a land of such cultural and geological diversity that it is often referred to as "all of Africa in one triangle" (referring to the country's triangular shape). From the near-desert regions of the extreme north to the lush rain forest of the south to the rolling volcanic hills of the west, more than two hundred distinct ethnic groups, each with its own beliefs and customs, call Cameroon their home. Christian and Muslim traditions thrive side by side with a belief in ancestral spirits that guide and protect the local population.

Bitterleaf stew, or *ndolé*, is the national dish of Cameroon. It originated with the Douala people of the Atlantic coast and is often eaten at times of celebration in honor of one's ancestors.

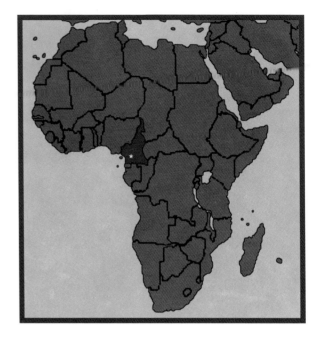

## BITTERLEAF STEW

**To make this recipe easier to prepare, I have substituted spinach for the bitterleaf. Kale can also be used instead of bitterleaf.**

2  pounds spinach

½ cup *egusi* (pumpkin seeds), de-hulled and ground,
    or peanut butter

6  tablespoons peanut oil

4  tomatoes, peeled and chopped

1  medium onion, chopped

3  cloves of garlic (about 1 tablespoon), crushed

1  knuckle of ginger (about 2 tablespoon), peeled and finely chopped

1 heaping tablespoon dried *njanga* (shrimp), ground, or shrimp
    paste (both available in African or Asian speciality markets)

⅔ cup water

hot-pepper sauce, to taste

salt, to taste

With the help of an adult, cut the spinach into thin slices and place it in a large bowl. Bring a pot of water to boil. Place the whole tomatoes into the boiling water for 30 seconds, then remove them with a slotted spoon and plunge them into cold water. This will make them easier to peel. Pour the rest of the boiling water over the spinach, then immediately pour off the water. When it has cooled, press the leaves to remove excess water. Set aside. Mix the *egusi* in a bowl with enough water to form a paste. Set aside. Heat the peanut oil in a heavy-bottomed saucepan and add the tomatoes, onion, garlic, ginger, and dried shrimp. Mix well and sauté for 10 minutes, stirring frequently. Add the *egusi* paste, water, hot-pepper sauce, and salt. Cook for approximately 10 minutes. Stir in the spinach and cook uncovered until tender, stirring often. Serve with rice. Cubes of fried beef or fish may be added to the top of the stew.

*Feeds 4 regular people or one hungry god.*